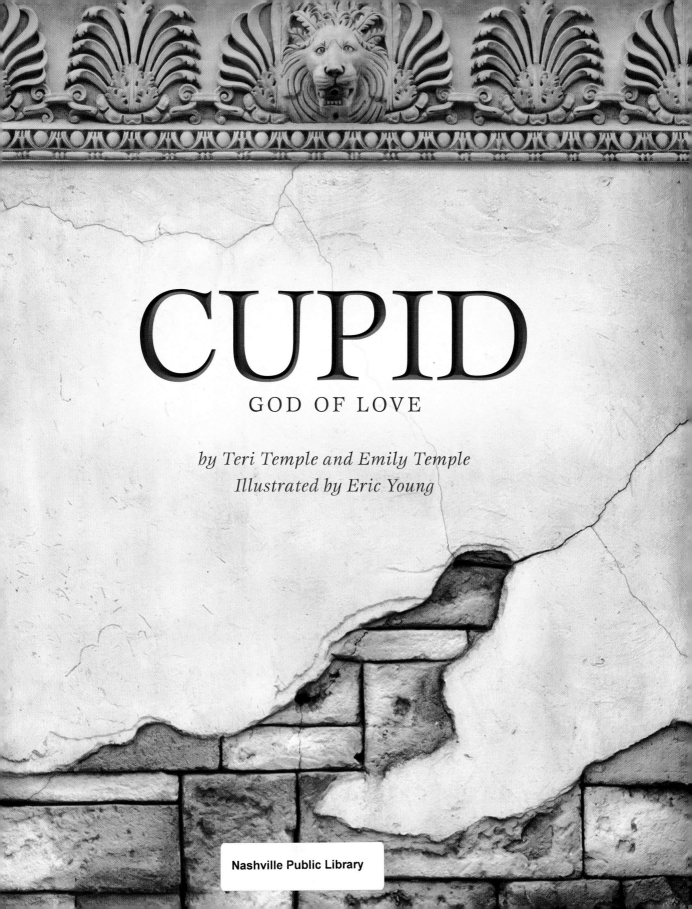

# CUPID

## GOD OF LOVE

*by Teri Temple and Emily Temple*
*Illustrated by Eric Young*

Published by The Child's World®
1980 Lookout Drive • Mankato, MN 56003-1705
800-599-READ • www.childsworld.com

ACKNOWLEDGMENTS
The Child's World®: Mary Berendes, Publishing Director
Red Line Editorial: Editorial direction
The Design Lab: Design and production
Design elements ©: Banana Republic Images/Shutterstock Images; Shutterstock
Images; Anton Balazh/Shutterstock Images
Photographs ©: Viacheslav Lopatin/Shutterstock Images, 5; Léon Bazille Per-
rault, 8; Zvonimir Atletic/Shutterstock Images, 12; Renata Sedmakova/Shut-
terstock Images, 22; LiliGraphie/Shutterstock Images, 26; Konstantin Yolshin/
Shutterstock Images, 28

ISBN 9781631437151
LCCN 2014945396

Printed in the United States of America
Mankato, MN
November, 2014
PA02241

# TABLE *of* CONTENTS

# INTRODUCTION

In ancient times Romans believed in spirits or gods called numina. In Latin, *numina* means divine will or power. The Romans took part in religious rituals to please the gods. They felt the gods had powers that could make their lives better.

As the Roman government grew more powerful, its armies conquered many neighboring lands. Romans often adopted beliefs from these new cultures. They greatly admired the Greek arts and sciences. Gradually, the Romans combined the Greek myths and religion with their own. These stories shaped and influenced each part of a Roman citizen's daily life. Ancient Roman poets, such as Ovid and Virgil, wrote down these tales of wonder. Their writings became a part of Rome's great history. To the Romans, however, these stories were not just for entertainment. Roman mythology was their key to understanding the world.

**ANCIENT ROMAN SOCIETIES**
Ancient Roman society was divided into several groups. The patricians were the most powerful and wealthiest group. They often owned land and held power in the government. The plebeians worked for the patricians. Slaves were prisoners of war or children without parents. Some slaves were freed and enjoyed most of the rights of citizens.

# CHARACTERS AND PLACES

ANCIENT ROME

ADRIATIC SEA

ROME

TYRRHENIAN SEA

**TROJAN WAR:**
*War between the ancient
Greeks and Trojans*

**MOUNT OLYMPUS**
*(mount uh-lim-PUHs)*:
*The mountaintop home
of the Olympic gods*

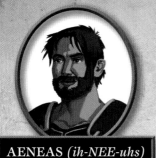

### AENEAS *(ih-NEE-uhs)*

*Hero of the Trojan War; son of Anchises and Venus; founder of Rome*

### APOLLO *(a-POL-lo)*

*God of Sun, music, healing, and prophecy; son of Jupiter and Latona; twin to Diana*

### CUPID *(KYOO-pid)*

*God of love; son of Venus; one of original gods at beginning of creation*

### DAPHNE *(DAF-nee)*

*Nymph who was transformed into a laurel tree to escape Apollo*

### DIDO *(DAHY-doh)*

*Queen of Carthage who killed herself when abandoned by Aeneas*

### JASON *(JEY-suhn)*

*Greek hero who led the Argonauts on a quest to find the Golden Fleece*

### MEDEA *(meh-DEE-uh)*

*Sorceress wife of Greek hero Jason; helped him obtain the Golden Fleece*

### PSYCHE *(SY-kee)*

*Goddess of the soul; wife of Cupid; originally a mortal*

### VENUS *(VEE-nuhs)*

*Goddess of love and beauty; born of sea foam; wife of Vulcan; mother of Cupid*

# THE GOD OF LOVE

Ancient Romans called on Cupid for love. Cupid was the Roman god of love and desire. He is part of both Roman and Greek mythologies. The Greeks called him Eros. He is regarded as the most beautiful of all the gods in both traditions.

Many of the Roman gods have interesting birth stories. Cupid's birth story is mysterious. There are several versions of his story. He has different parents in each one. In most of the stories, Cupid's mother is Venus, the goddess of love. In one of the legends, his father is Mars, the god of war. Others state Cupid's father is Mercury, the messenger to the gods, or even Jupiter. Some even say Cupid was born from a silver egg.

### EROS

Eros, the Greek god of love, and Cupid were very similar. When the myths of the two cultures combined, the stories of Eros and Cupid mixed together. In the 5th century BCE, the Greek playwright Aristophanes wrote a story of Eros's birth. Aristophanes thought Eros was the son of the gods of night and darkness. Together these gods Nox and Erebus created an egg. When it hatched, Eros came out of it. His birth brought light and love into the world.

One detail about every story is the same. Cupid is often shown as a baby with wings. He carries a bow and arrows. He can shoot his arrows at gods and mortals and make them fall in love. He is often thought of as mischievous in his matchmaking. But most Romans and Greeks thought of him fondly. They thought Cupid brought them love.

Ancient Romans believed Venus formed when the body parts of Caelus mixed with sea foam. Venus rose from the sea. She was the most beautiful creature in heaven or on Earth. She became the goddess of love and beauty. One legend claims that two cherubs were born with Venus. A cherub is an angel in the form of a winged baby. These cherubs, Cupid and Himeros, were her attendants. They were the gods of love and desire.

In later myths, poets wrote that Cupid was the son of Venus and Mars. Mars, the mighty god of war, was not Venus's husband. Venus was married to Mars's brother, Vulcan, the god of fire. But Vulcan was ugly. Venus's true love was the handsome Mars. But it was Vulcan who crafted Cupid's special arrows. Regardless of who Cupid's parents truly were, he was always loyal to Venus.

Cupid was the youngest of all the
gods. He was charming and beautiful.
But he was also mischievous. The
gods knew him for his naughty and
sometimes cruel tricks. He often stole
weapons from the gods and mortal
heroes. He even stole Jupiter's
thunderbolts.

**VALENTINE'S DAY**
Cupid is often associated with
Valentine's Day. Valentine was
an ancient Roman priest and
a romantic. He performed
marriages for soldiers and
their wives in secret against the
emperor's decree. As a result, he
was put to death on February 14.
It became a day to remember
Saint Valentine.

Cupid spent most of his time
matchmaking amongst the gods
and humans. He enjoyed flying
around with his bow and arrows
at the ready. Shots from his
arrows did not hurt. He had two
types of arrows. One kind had gold tips. The gold-tipped
arrows inspired love in the people they hit. His other
arrows were made of lead. People struck by a lead arrow
grew to hate one another. Cupid loved to watch the events
unfold from above.

One victim of Cupid's tricks was Apollo. Apollo was the mighty god of the Sun. He liked to tease Cupid about his archery skills. Apollo thought he was a much better archer than Cupid. His teasing made Cupid mad. So Cupid decided to play a trick on Apollo's heart.

Cupid fired two arrows. First he hit Apollo with the golden arrow of love. Then Cupid shot a lead arrow at a beautiful nymph named Daphne. Apollo fell in love with Daphne instantly. But because of the lead arrow, Daphne had no interest in loving anyone. Apollo was so in love with Daphne that he chased her all through the woods. He tried to convince her that he was worthy of her love. Daphne only ignored him.

Apollo finally caught up with Daphne. Just as he reached out to her, Daphne begged her father Ladon, a river god, for help. Daphne's father turned her into a laurel tree. She was instantly covered in bark and grew roots into the ground. Apollo was heartbroken. He vowed to never forget Daphne. The laurel became his sacred tree.

Cupid's next victim was Jason. Jason was a Greek hero and the son of a king. When Jason was a young boy, his uncle Pelias took over the throne from Jason's father. When he grew older, Jason wanted to claim his birthright as king.

Pelias agreed to hand over the kingdom to Jason on one condition. Jason would have to travel to Colchis and retrieve the Golden Fleece. Jupiter, the king of the gods, had once owned the fleece. King Aeetes now owned it. He kept the fleece heavily guarded. Jason knew it would be a very dangerous mission, but he agreed. Jason took 50 warriors with him. They set sail on a ship called the *Argo*. They were known as the Argonauts.

On their journey, the Argonauts faced many challenges. They fought ferocious, sharp-clawed monsters called Harpies. They sailed through clashing rocks. When they finally arrived at Colchis, Jason and the Argonauts thought their trials were over. They were wrong.

Jason and the Argonauts met King Aeetes. Jason offered his service in exchange for the fleece. King Aeetes did not like Jason and his men. Secretly, he wanted to kill them all. But he agreed to give Jason the fleece.

In return, King Aeetes wanted Jason to plow his fields with fire-breathing bulls. When that was done, Jason was to sow the fields with dragons' teeth. It was hard and dangerous work. Aeetes didn't think Jason could do it. But he didn't know Jason had the goddess Juno on his side.

Juno knew the only person who could help Jason was a sorceress named Medea. Medea was also King Aeetes's daughter. Juno asked Venus for help. Venus sent Cupid to make Medea fall in love with Jason. She knew Cupid's gold-tipped arrows would do the trick.

While Medea was under Cupid's love spell, she agreed to help Jason. Medea betrayed her father by giving Jason a lotion. The lotion protected him from the bulls. Jason then sowed the dragon teeth, but they grew into armed warriors. Medea made Jason and his weapons invisible so he could fight the warriors. Finally she led Jason to the

Golden Fleece. Medea cast a spell on the fleece's guardian dragon. While it was sleeping, Jason snatched up the fleece. He sailed away with his prize and Medea. For once, Cupid's meddling worked.

Cupid then played a role in one very famous love story. The story began with the goddesses Juno, Minerva, and Venus. All three were arguing about who was the most beautiful. Jupiter could not decide, so he enlisted the help of Paris.

Paris was a prince from the city of Troy. Each goddess wanted Paris to choose her. Each bribed Paris with rewards. Juno offered Paris power. Minerva offered him wisdom. But Venus knew what Paris really wanted. She promised Paris the most beautiful woman in the world as his wife. That woman was Helen.

Paris chose Venus as the winner. But there was one small problem. Helen was already married to the king of Sparta. Venus asked Cupid to help get Helen away from her husband. So Cupid shot Helen with a gold-tipped arrow. She instantly fell in love with Paris and agreed to leave Greece with him. Her husband thought Helen had been kidnapped. Furious, the king of Sparta sent out a Greek army to bring her back. The Trojan War began. After ten years, the Greek army overtook Troy. Paris was killed in the battle, and Helen had to go back to the king. Cupid's meddling did not always have a happy ending.

Cupid continued to meddle. One of the heroes of the Trojan War was Aeneas. He would go on to found Rome. Following the war, Aeneas and the surviving Trojans fled Troy. They sailed toward Italy. As they approached shore, a giant storm crossed their path. The strong storm pushed them off course, all the way to Carthage. When they arrived, Dido, the queen of Carthage, welcomed them with open arms.

**JULIUS CAESAR**
Julius Caesar was a famous statesman in ancient Rome. Ancient Romans believed he was a descendent of Ascanius. Since Ascanius was the grandson of Venus, Julius Caesar could trace his roots back to a goddess. Caesar helped build ancient Rome into a mighty empire. A group of nobles killed him while he was trying to make changes in the Roman government.

Aeneas told Dido of their many trials. He told her the Greeks had invaded and destroyed the city, causing them to flee. He, his father, and his son, Ascanius, had decided to sail for Italy because the gods told Aeneas a glorious future awaited him there.

Dido threw the Trojans a massive feast. Aeneas called a servant to bring Ascanius to the party. Venus decided

to intervene. She asked Cupid to disguise himself as
Ascanius in order to inflame Dido with love for Aeneas.
Cupid took on the form of Ascanius and shot Dido with a
golden arrow. Dido fell head over heels for Aeneas.

Dido and Aeneas lived together for many years. Then
the gods reminded Aeneas he was to found the city of
Rome. Dido was so saddened by his departure that she
killed herself. Cupid's meddling again ended badly.

Cupid spent most of his time involved in the love affairs of others. He only fell victim to the spell of his own arrows once. In ancient times there lived a king who had three lovely daughters. The most beautiful of the three was Psyche. People came from all over to admire her beauty. They admired her so much they forgot to worship Venus. A jealous goddess, Venus pleaded with her son Cupid to help her get revenge. Venus wanted Psyche to fall in love with a horrendous creature. But when Cupid saw Psyche, he immediately fell in love. It was the first time Cupid was the one in love.

Despite all of her admirers, no one would marry Psyche. Her parents asked the gods for advice. Apollo told them she was destined to marry a monster. He told them they should leave her on a mountaintop. The king and queen trusted the gods. They took Psyche to the top of a mountain. From there, the west wind lifted Psyche and placed her outside a grand mansion. Cupid visited Psyche here, but only at night. In the dark Psyche couldn't see his true form. And because Apollo told Psyche's parents so, she thought Cupid was a monster. But Psyche loved Cupid. She wanted to see his face. So one night she lit a lamp while Cupid was sleeping. She was shocked to find her husband was the god of love. Cupid was angry that Psyche did not trust him. He fled, leaving Psyche.

Psyche vowed to roam the earth until she found Cupid. She prayed to the gods for help. None of them would help her. Cupid had gone to Mount Olympus and told his mother the whole story. The gods were afraid of angering Venus further. The only way Psyche was going to win Cupid back was to go straight to Venus herself.

Psyche went to Venus and asked for her help. Determined to teach Psyche a lesson, Venus created a series of tasks for her to complete. Venus hoped Psyche would fail. First Venus covered the floor with the tiniest seeds. She told Psyche she had until morning to gather them all. Psyche thought the task would be impossible. But ants took pity on her and helped her.

Venus came up with several more impossible tasks. Psyche managed to accomplish each one.

MYTH OR FAIRYTALE
Could ancient mythology have influenced our fairy tales? The tales of Beauty and the Beast and Cinderella both have parts of the Cupid and Psyche myth. For example, Psyche thought she had married a beast, and she had to perform tasks for an evil mother figure. These stories of love and its trials can be found in all cultures throughout history.

Finally Cupid took pity on Psyche. He realized how much Psyche loved him. Cupid asked Jupiter for his permission to marry her. Jupiter agreed, and Psyche and Cupid lived happily ever after.

The angelic Cupid we picture today emerged from combining Greek and Roman stories. A Roman scholar named Cicero wrote about a statue of Cupid that was sculpted by Praxiteles, an ancient Greek sculptor. The statue was put in a small temple. People went to the shrine to worship Cupid alongside the hero Hercules.

In ancient times, these temples were used both for worship and to house great works of art. During the reign of the emperor Augustus, Cupid became a more prominent figure in Roman art. Augustus had defeated the forces of Anthony and Cleopatra in the Battle of Actium. Anthony and Cleopatra fled to Egypt. Augustus often symbolized his war victories with an image of Cupid transferring weapons from Mars to his mother Venus.

## CLEOPATRA

Cleopatra was the queen of Egypt. She has long been a fascinating figure in history. As beautiful as she was smart, Cleopatra used both attributes to make her country powerful. She asked Rome to help her. Two of its important leaders, Julius Caesar and Mark Antony, both fell in love with her. It didn't help. Egypt would be defeated in war, and Cleopatra would die alone from a snake bite.

In ancient Roman tradition, Cupid represented the soul. The Romans buried their dead in a type of stone coffin called a sarcophagus. They often decorated the sarcophagi with Cupid's image. Today we remember Cupid most often on Valentine's Day. On this holiday that celebrates love, we remember the god of love. As he has in the past, Cupid is sure to inspire or meddle in love stories well into the future.

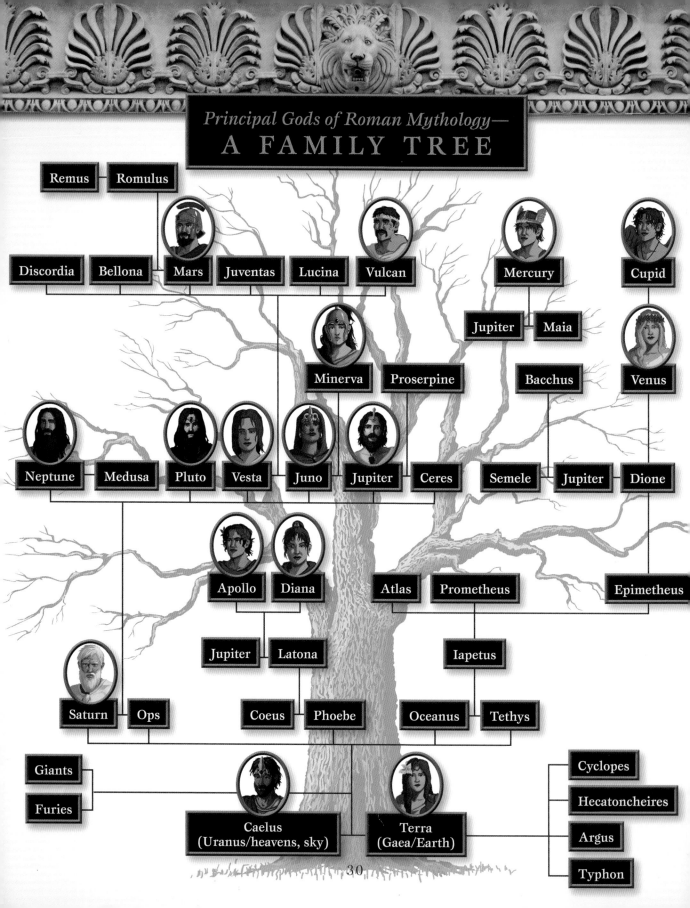

# Principal Gods of Roman Mythology—
# A FAMILY TREE

Remus — Romulus

Discordia — Bellona — Mars — Juventas — Lucina — Vulcan — Mercury — Cupid

Jupiter — Maia

Minerva — Proserpine — Bacchus — Venus

Neptune — Medusa — Pluto — Vesta — Juno — Jupiter — Ceres — Semele — Jupiter — Dione

Apollo — Diana — Atlas — Prometheus — Epimetheus

Jupiter — Latona — Iapetus

Saturn — Ops — Coeus — Phoebe — Oceanus — Tethys

Giants — Cyclopes

Furies — Hecatoncheires

Caelus (Uranus/heavens, sky) — Terra (Gaea/Earth) — Argus

Typhon

Ancient Greeks believed gods and goddesses ruled the world. The gods fell in love and struggled for power, but they never died. The ancient Greeks believed their gods were immortal. The Greek people worshiped the gods in temples. They felt the gods would protect and guide them. Over time, the Romans and many other cultures adopted the Greek myths as their own. While these other cultures changed the names of the gods, many of the stories remain the same.

**SATURN:** *Cronus*
*God of Time and God of Sowing*
*Symbol: Sickle or Scythe*

**JUPITER:** *Zeus*
*King of the Gods, God of Sky, Rain, and Thunder*
*Symbols: Thunderbolt, Eagle, and Oak Tree*

**JUNO:** *Hera*
*Queen of the Gods, Goddess of Marriage,*
*    Pregnancy, and Childbirth*
*Symbols: Peacock, Cow, and Diadem*
*    (Diamond Crown)*

**NEPTUNE:** *Poseidon*
*God of the Sea*
*Symbols: Trident, Horse, and Dolphin*

**PLUTO:** *Hades*
*God of the Underworld*
*Symbols: Invisibility Helmet and Pomegranate*

**MINERVA:** *Athena*
*Goddess of Wisdom, War, and Arts and Crafts*
*Symbols: Owl, Shield, Loom, and Olive Tree*

**MARS:** *Ares*
*God of War*
*Symbols: Wild Boar, Vulture, and Dog*

**DIANA:** *Artemis*
*Goddess of the Moon and Hunt*
*Symbols: Deer, Moon, and Silver Bow and Arrows*

**APOLLO:** *Apollo*
*God of the Sun, Music, Healing, and Prophecy*
*Symbols: Laurel Tree, Lyre, Bow, and Raven*

**VENUS:** *Aphrodite*
*Goddess of Love and Beauty*
*Symbols: Dove, Swan, and Rose*

**CUPID:** *Eros*
*God of Love*
*Symbols: Bow and Arrows*

**MERCURY:** *Hermes*
*Messenger to the Gods, God of Travelers and Trade*
*Symbols: Crane, Caduceus, Winged Sandals,*
*    and Helmet*

# FURTHER INFORMATION

### BOOKS

Johnson, Robin. *Understanding Roman Myths*. New York: Crabtree Publishing, 2012.

Temple, Teri. *Apollo: God of the Sun, Healing, Music, and Poetry*. Mankato, MN: Child's World, 2013.

Wolfson, Evelyn. *Mythology of the Romans*. Berkeley Heights, NJ: Enslow, 2014.

### WEB SITES

Visit our Web site for links about Cupid: *childsworld.com/links*

*Note to Parents, Teachers, and Librarians: We routinely verify our Web links to make sure they are safe and active sites. So encourage your readers to check them out!*

# INDEX